A Treasure's Trove
Wings and Rings

Written and Illustrated by Michael Stadther

Published in the United States by Treasure Trove, Inc.
161 Cherry Street, New Canaan, CT 06840

Distributed by Simon Scribbles
An imprint of Simon & Schuster Children's Publishing Division
1230 Avenue of the Americas, New York, NY 10020

Visit www.atreasurestrove.com or www.alchemistdar.com
for information about the treasure hunt and the next book.

Manufactured in the United States of America

First Edition
2 4 6 8 10 9 7 5 3 1

ISBN-13: 978-0-9760618-9-2
ISBN-10: 0-9760618-9-9

Match the Rings

The fairies are looking for rings.
Circle the two rings that match.

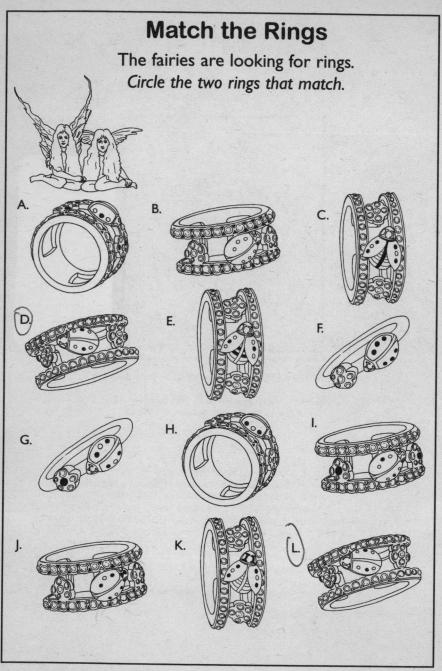

A.

B.

C.

D.

E.

F.

G.

H.

I.

J.

K.

L.

Match the Fairy

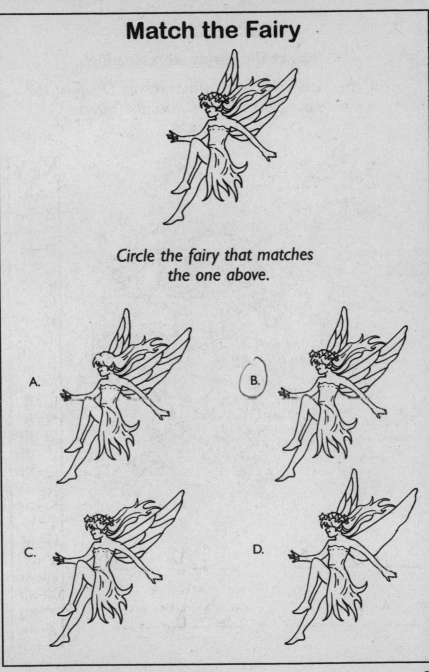

Circle the fairy that matches
the one above.

A.

B.

C.

D.

Morse Code

What are the fairies searching for?

Read the Morse code in the mushrooms. Decipher the code using the key and write the letters in the spaces.

START

KEY

A –∙∣
B –∣∙∙∙
C –∣∙∣∙
D –∣∙∙
E –∙
F –∙∙∣∙
G –∣∣∙
H –∙∙∙∙
I –∙∙
J –∙∣∣∣
K ∣∙∣
L –∙∣∙∙
M –∣∣
N –∣∙
O –∣∣∣
P –∙∣∣∙
Q –∣∣∙∣
R –∙∣∙
S –∙∙∙
T –∣
U –∙∙∣
V –∙∙∙∣
W –∙∣∣
X –∣∙∙∣
Y –∣∙∣∣
Z –∣∣∙∙

THEIR   HIDDEN

FAIRY   RINGS

4

Connect the Dots

Draw the fairy by connecting the dots.

Rings Maze

Draw lines through the maze from each fairy to her ring.

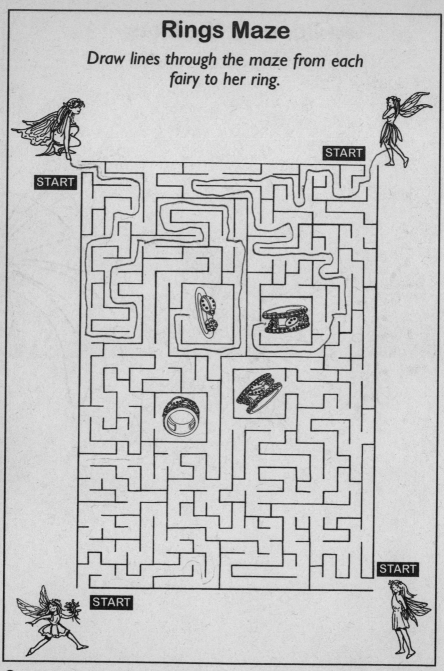

START

START

START

START

Which One Is Different?

Circle the fairy that is different
from the others.

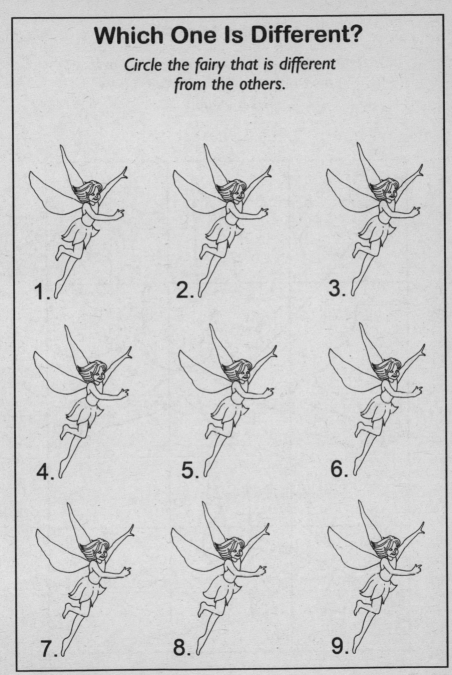

1.

2.

3.

4.

5.

6.

7.

8.

9.

Complete the Fairy

Draw the missing pieces in the empty boxes on the next page, using the picture below as a guide.

Connect the Dots

Draw the Kootenstoopit by connecting the dots.

Find the Fairies

*Circle the six fairies
hidden in the leaves.*

Match the Shadows

*Draw a line from each Kootenstoopit
to his shadow.*

Flower Maze

Draw a line through the flower maze from the
fairy to her friends.

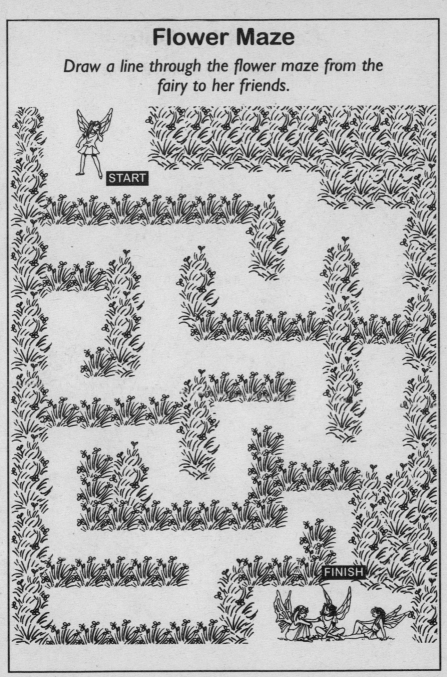

START

FINISH

Connect the Dots

Draw the Pickensrooter by connecting the dots.

Celestial Word Search

Find and circle the hidden words in any direction.

PLANETS **SOLAR** **LUNAR** **SUN**

SYZYGY **MOON** **STARS** **ECLIPSE**

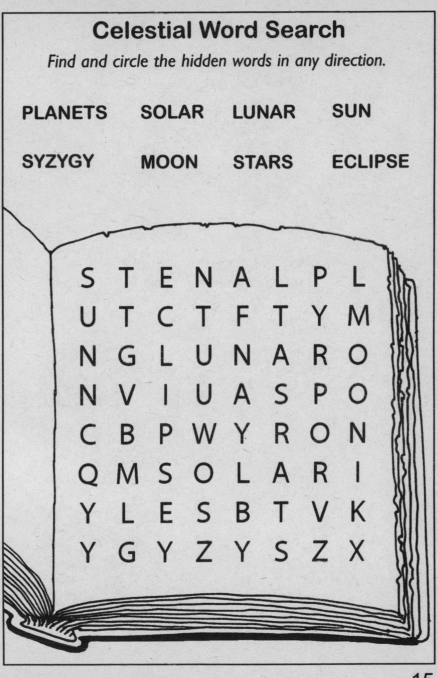

```
S T E N A L P L
U T C T F T Y M
N G L U N A R O
N V I U A S P O
C B P W Y R O N
Q M S O L A R I
Y L E S B T V K
Y G Y Z Y S Z X
```

Match the Kootenstoopit

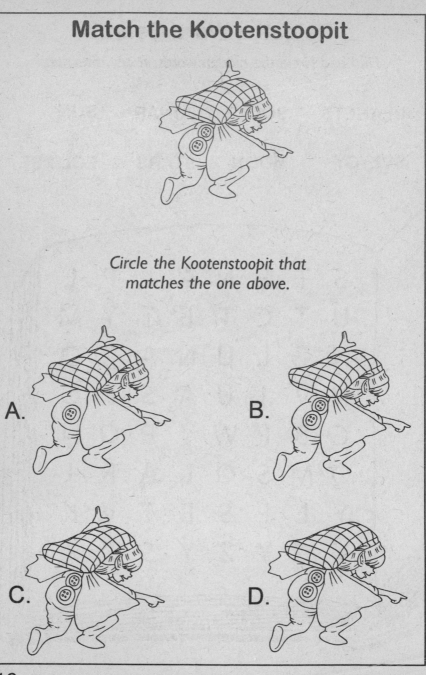

*Circle the Kootenstoopit that
matches the one above.*

A.

B.

C.

D.

16

Find the Path

Circle the letter of the line that leads to the Pickensrooter.

Word Jumble

What are the fairies holding?

Unscramble the letters and write them in the spaces to discover the answer.

LFOWRSE

_ _ _ _ _ _ _

Connect the Dots

Draw the fairy by connecting the dots.

Fairies Maze

Draw a line through the maze from each fairy to the jewel.

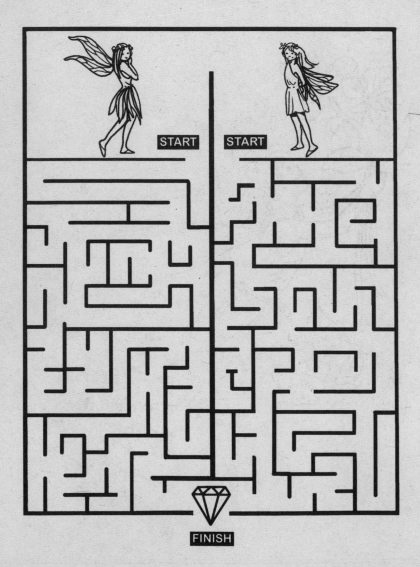

START   START

FINISH

Match the Shadows

Draw a line from each Pickensrooter
to his shadow.

Ring Maze

*Draw a line through the maze from
the fairy to her ring.*

START

FINISH

Match the Shadows

*Draw a line from each fairy
to her shadow.*

Secret Message

Unscramble the letters below to get a hint for a clue in the book Secrets of the Alchemist Dar.

*Look on page 100
for GRNODYLAF*

— — — — — — — —

Find the Path

Circle the letter of the line that leads to the Kootenstoopit.

Secret Code

Why does a fairy need her ring?

Match the numbers to the letters in the key and write the letters in the spaces to decipher the answer.

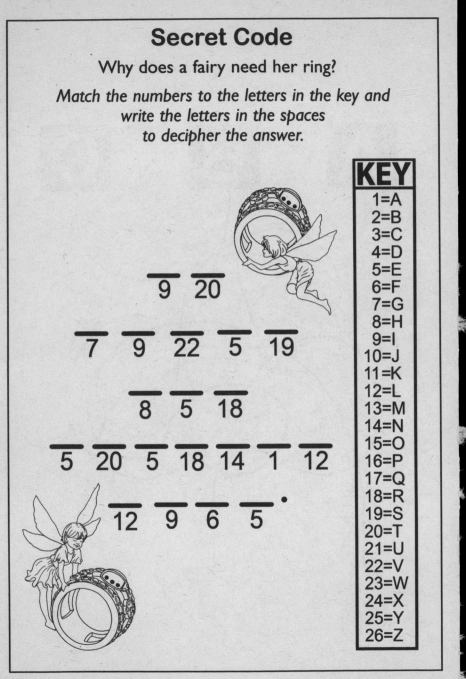

$\overline{9}\ \overline{20}$

$\overline{7}\ \overline{9}\ \overline{22}\ \overline{5}\ \overline{19}$

$\overline{8}\ \overline{5}\ \overline{18}$

$\overline{5}\ \overline{20}\ \overline{5}\ \overline{18}\ \overline{14}\ \overline{1}\ \overline{12}$

$\overline{12}\ \overline{9}\ \overline{6}\ \overline{5}$.

KEY

1=A	14=N
2=B	15=O
3=C	16=P
4=D	17=Q
5=E	18=R
6=F	19=S
7=G	20=T
8=H	21=U
9=I	22=V
10=J	23=W
11=K	24=X
12=L	25=Y
13=M	26=Z

Match the Pickensrooter

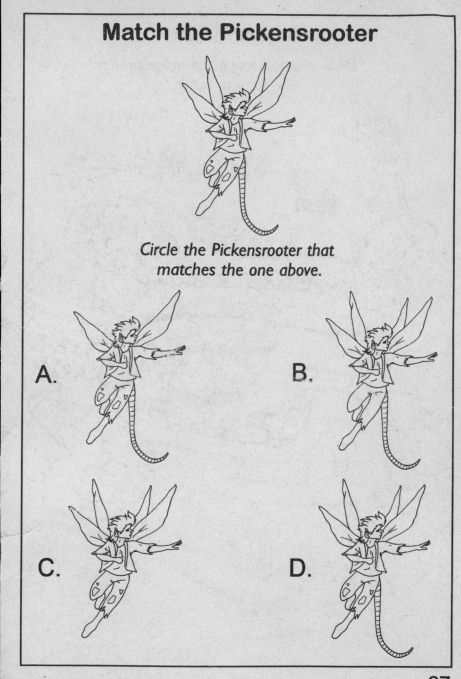

*Circle the Pickensrooter that
matches the one above.*

A.

B.

C.

D.

27

Yorah Maze

Draw a line through the maze from
the fairy to Yorah.

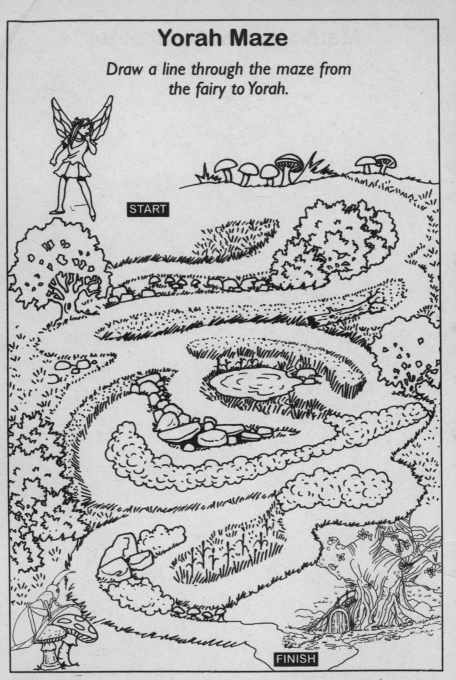

START

FINISH

Connect the Dots

Draw the Kootenstoopit by connecting the dots.

Number Maze

Draw a line following the even numbers through the number maze from start to finish.

START

2	6	3	15	23	55	33	51	3	21
9	8	1	25	37	29	13	5	9	33
5	12	16	11	9	17	26	42	8	47
11	19	4					1	2	41
14	20	10					3	4	5
28	21	15					21	32	9
30	7	33					5	18	10
22	26	24	6	27	7	9	23	11	12
37	17	23	3	49	41	5	15	3	4
41	13	9	1	21	11	17	25	51	10

FINISH

30

Connect the Dots

*Draw the jewel by
connecting the dots.*

Complete the Fairy

Draw the missing pieces in the empty boxes on the next page, using the picture below as a guide.

Flower Maze

Draw a line through the maze from the fairy to her friends.

Connect the Dots

Draw the fairy by connecting the dots.

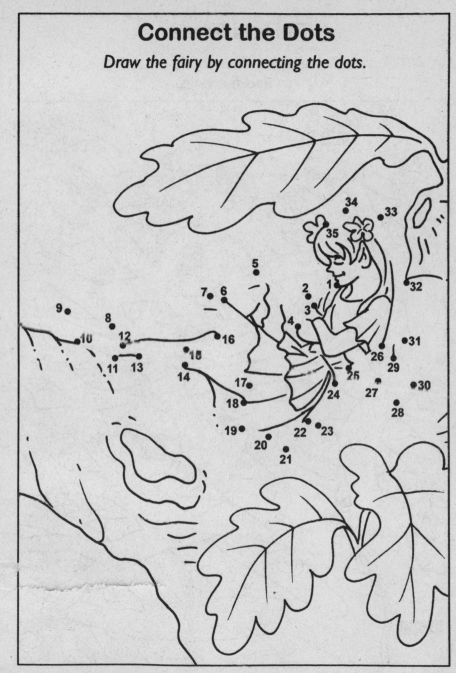

Rings Maze

Draw a line through the maze
to find five rings.

Find the Path

Circle the letter of the line that leads to
the fairy.

Fairy Maze

Draw a line through the maze from the fairy to the cave.

38

Forest Path Word Search

Find and circle the hidden words in any direction.

```
Y O R A H O W
J R K L B N O
C I I Q E A L
B G P A T H L
F H J K F O O
K T A D Y M F
R E V Z W E L
```

FOLLOW	HOME	RIGHT
PATH	YORAH	FAIRY

Which One Is Different?

*Circle the fairy that is different
from the others.*

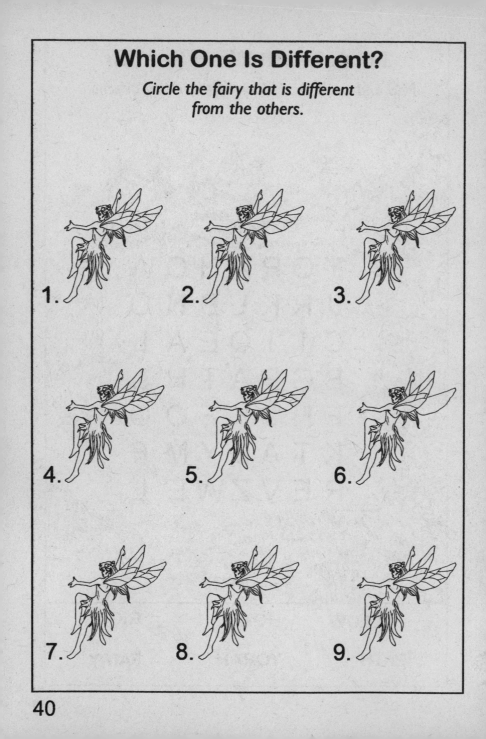

1.

2.

3.

4.

5.

6.

7.

8.

9.

Match the Shadow

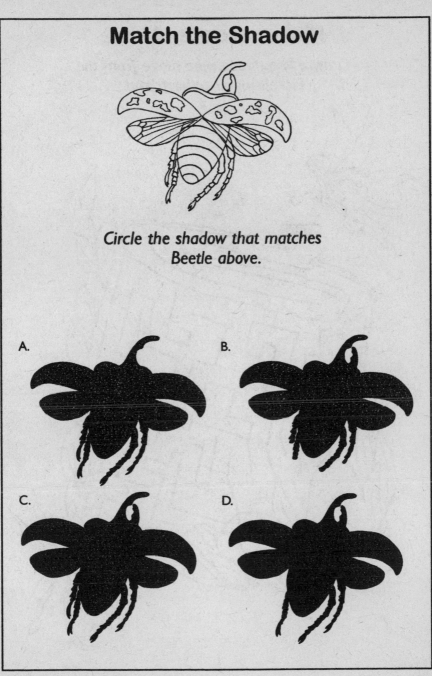

Circle the shadow that matches
Beetle above.

A.

B.

C.

D.

Pickensrooter Maze

Draw a line through the maze from the
Pickensrooter to his friend.

Treasure Hunt

Find where the fairy ring is hidden by following the instructions.

1. Draw a line between two fairies that are exactly alike.

2. Next draw a line between two Forest Creatures that are exactly alike.

3. Circle the place where the lines cross— this is where the ring is hidden.

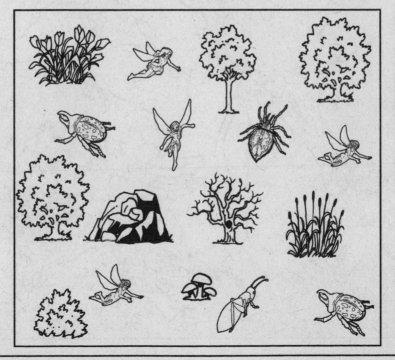

Find the Differences

Circle at least eight things added to the picture on the following page.

Secret Code

What special gifts do Pickensrooters have?

Match the numbers to the letters in the key and write the letters in the spaces to decipher the answer.

16 9 3 11

12 15 3 11 19

1 14 4

21 14 20 9 5

18 9 2 2 15 14 19

KEY

1=A
2=B
3=C
4=D
5=E
6=F
7=G
8=H
9=I
10=J
11=K
12=L
13=M
14=N
15=O
16=P
17=Q
18=R
19=S
20=T
21=U
22=V
23=W
24=X
25=Y
26=Z

46

Match the Shadow

*Circle the shadow that belongs to
the Pickensrooter above.*

A.

B.

C.

D.

Leaf Maze

Draw lines through the leaf maze from each fairy to her mushroom.

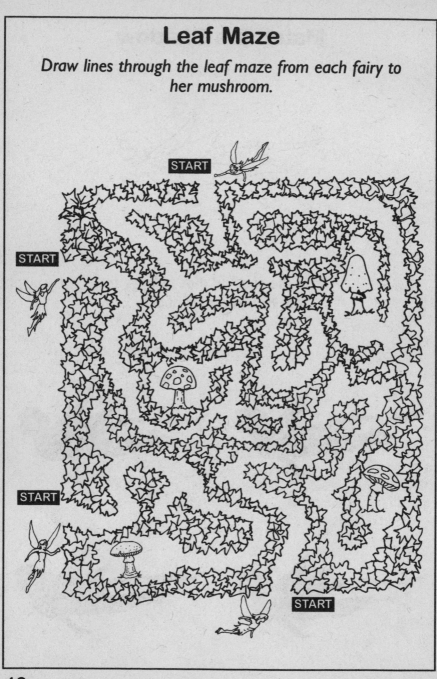

Match the Shadow

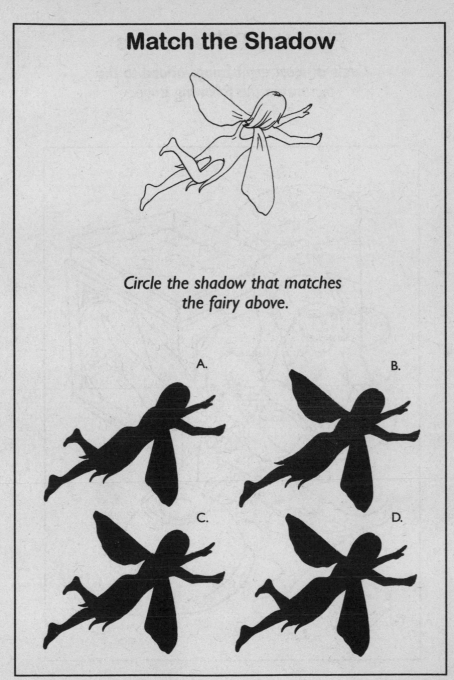

*Circle the shadow that matches
the fairy above.*

A.

B.

C.

D.

Find the Differences

Circle at least eight things added to the picture on the following page.

Jewel Maze

Draw a line through the maze from the fairy past the jewels hidden in the knotholes to the finish.

FINISH

START

Treasure Hunt

Help the fairy find her lost ring by following the instructions.

1. Draw a line between two letters that are exactly alike.

2. Next draw a line between two numbers that are exactly alike.

3. Circle the place where the lines cross— you've found the fairy's lost ring!

3

A

F

2

C

4

8

6

A

2

Rose Maze

*Draw a line through the maze from
the fairy to the jewel.*

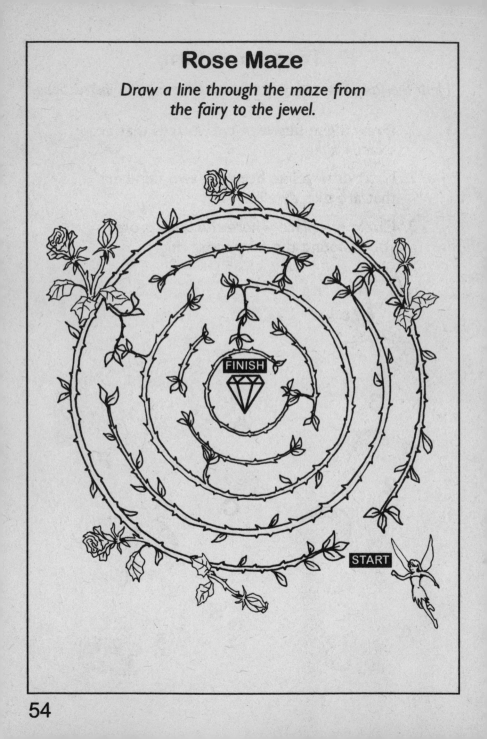

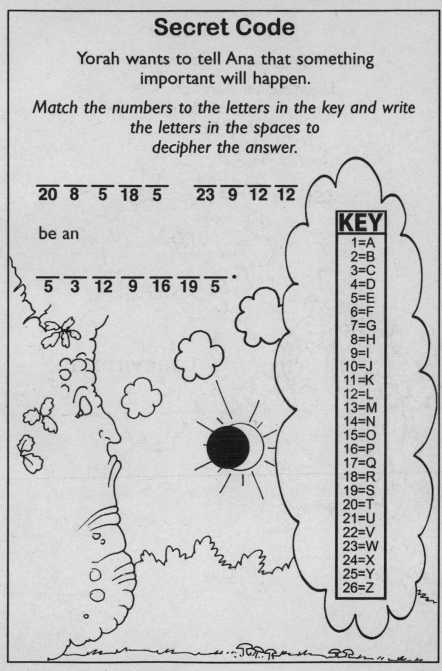

Secret Code

Yorah wants to tell Ana that something important will happen.

Match the numbers to the letters in the key and write the letters in the spaces to decipher the answer.

$\overline{20}$ $\overline{8}$ $\overline{5}$ $\overline{18}$ $\overline{5}$ $\overline{23}$ $\overline{9}$ $\overline{12}$ $\overline{12}$

be an

$\overline{5}$ $\overline{3}$ $\overline{12}$ $\overline{9}$ $\overline{16}$ $\overline{19}$ $\overline{5}$.

KEY

1=A
2=B
3=C
4=D
5=E
6=F
7=G
8=H
9=I
10=J
11=K
12=L
13=M
14=N
15=O
16=P
17=Q
18=R
19=S
20=T
21=U
22=V
23=W
24=X
25=Y
26=Z

Word Jumble

Ana is trying to send Zac her thoughts.

*Unjumble her words and write
them on the lines on the next page
to help Zac.*

Secret Code

Where do the fairies live?

Solve the math problems and write the answers in the leaves. Then write each answer's letter in the matching numbered space.

$4 +4$ **H**

$6 -3$ **A**

$12 -3$ **R**

$3 +3$ **S**

$15 -1$ **C**

$10 -8$ **O**

$6 +6$ **E**

$20 -7$ **A**

$25 -20$ **Y**

$9 -8$ **H**

$4 +3$ **B**

$6 +4$ **S**

$5 -1$ **R**

$7 +4$ **N**

,

___ ___ ___ ___ ___ ___
5   2   4   3   1   6

___ ___ ___ ___ ___ ___ ___ ___
7 9 13 11 14 8 12 10

58

Find the Kootenstoopits

Draw a line through the maze to outline three Kootenstoopits.

START

FINISH

Secret Code

What's in Zac's boot?

Solve the math problems and write the answers in the boots. Then write each answer's letter in the matching numbered spaces.

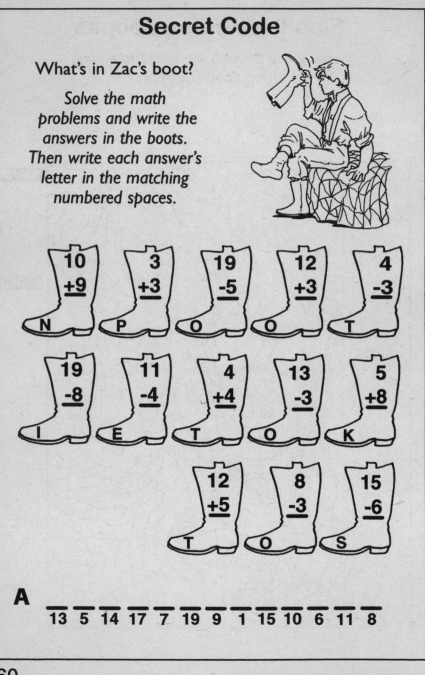

10 +9 N	3 +3 P	19 -5 O	12 +3 O	4 -3 T
19 -8 I	11 -4 E	4 +4 T	13 -3 O	5 +8 K
	12 +5 T	8 -3 O	15 -6 S	

A __ __ __ __ __ __ __ __ __ __ __ __ __
13 5 14 17 7 19 9 1 15 10 6 11 8

60

Answers

Page 2: D, L

Page 3: B

Page 4: THEIR HIDDEN FAIRY RINGS

Page 6:

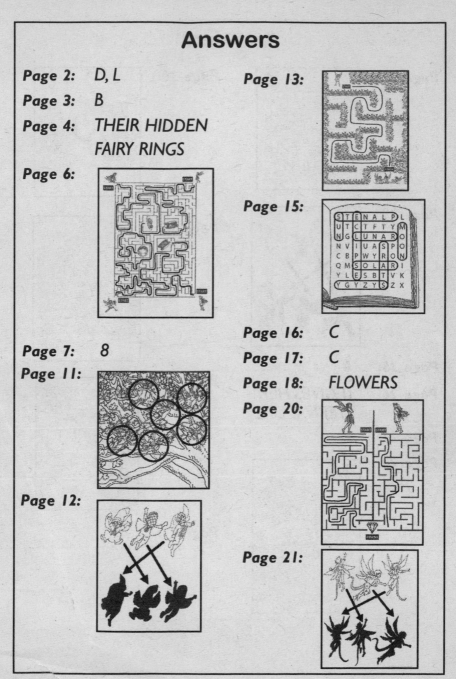

Page 7: 8

Page 11:

Page 12:

Page 13:

Page 15:

Page 16: C

Page 17: C

Page 18: FLOWERS

Page 20:

Page 21:

Answers

Page 22: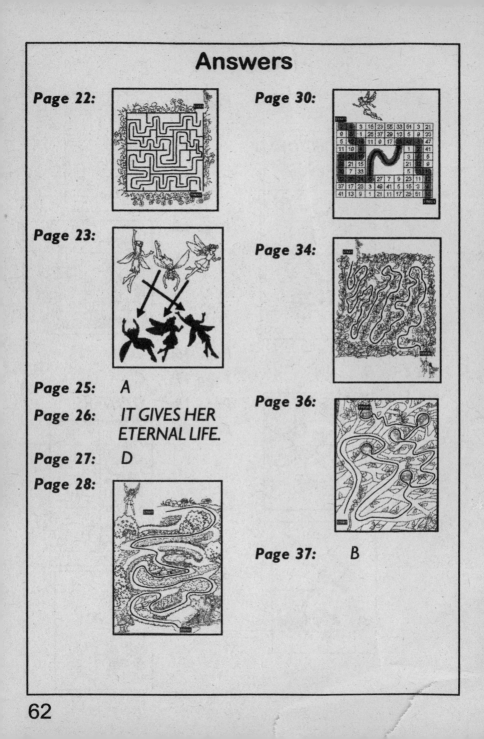

Page 23:

Page 25: A

Page 26: IT GIVES HER ETERNAL LIFE.

Page 27: D

Page 28:

Page 30:

Page 34:

Page 36:

Page 37: B

Answers

Page 38:

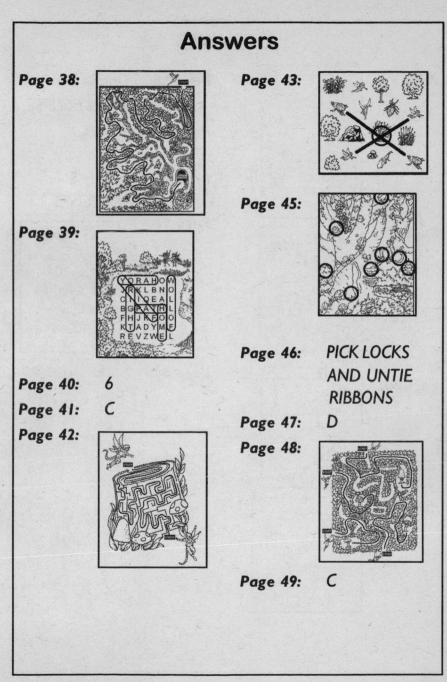

Page 39:

Page 40: 6

Page 41: C

Page 42:

Page 43:

Page 45:

Page 46: PICK LOCKS AND UNTIE RIBBONS

Page 47: D

Page 48:

Page 49: C

Answers

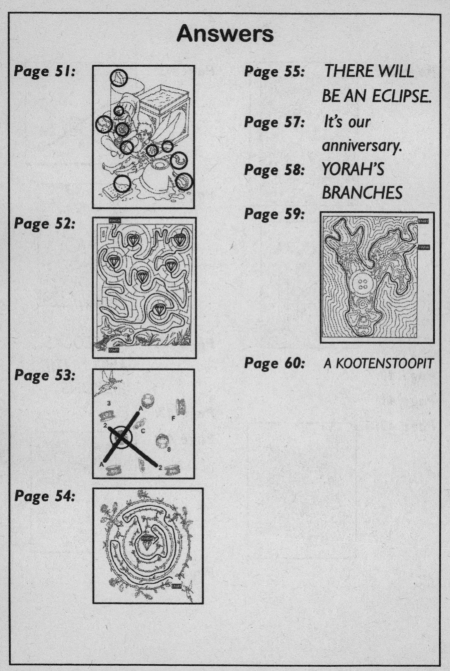

Page 51:

Page 52:

Page 53:

Page 54:

Page 55: THERE WILL BE AN ECLIPSE.

Page 57: It's our anniversary.

Page 58: YORAH'S BRANCHES

Page 59:

Page 60: A KOOTENSTOOPIT